P9-DXN-969

To _____

From _____

With Love

SAN RAMON

Froggie Went A-Courtin'

As told and illustrated by Iza Trapani

CONTRA COSTA COUNTY LIBRARY

WITHDRAWN

Whispering Coyote
A Charlesbridge Imprint

3 1901 03227 6240

Copyright © 2002 by Iza Trapani
All rights reserved, including the right of reproduction
in whole or in part in any form.
Charlesbridge, Whispering Coyote, and colophon are registered trademarks of
Charlesbridge Publishing.

A Whispering Coyote Book
Published by Charlesbridge Publishing
85 Main Street
Watertown, MA 02472
(617) 926-0329
www.charlesbridge.com

Library of Congress Cataloging-in-Publication Data
Trapani, Iza.
Froggie went a-courtin' / written and illustrated by Iza Trapani.
p. cm.
"A Whispering Coyote Book."
Summary: An adaptation of the folk song about a frog in search of a bride.
ISBN 1-58089-028-8 (hardcover)
1. Folk songs, English—Texts. [1. Folk songs.] I. Title.
PZ8.3.T686 Fr 2001
782.42162'21'00268—dc21
2001004376

Printed in China
10 9 8 7 6 5 4 3 2 1
The illustrations in this book were done in watercolors on
Arches 300 lb. cold press watercolor paper.
The display type and text type were set in Whimsey and 16 point Tiffany Medium.
Separated and manufactured by Jade Productions
Book production by *The Kids at Our House*
Designed by *The Kids at Our House*

For Lou,
who helped to make
my dream come true

Froggie went a-courtin', he did ride,
H'hm, h'hm.
Froggie went a-courtin', he did ride
With a rose and chocolates by his side,
H'hm, h'hm.

Froggie said to Mousie, "Marry me,
Oh yes, oh yes.
Be my little honey, my sweet pea;
What a caring husband I will be,
Oh yes, oh yes."

"I don't want a frog to hold and squeeze,
Oh no, oh no.
I don't like the water, you hate cheese,
So you might as well get off your knees,
Oh no, oh no."

Froggie said to Turtle, "Be my bride,
A-ha, a-ha.
Hurry up my darling, do decide,
For a love like ours can't be denied,
A-ha, a-ha."

Turtle shook her head, "You move too fast,
Uh-uh, uh-uh.
We don't need an expert to forecast
That our marriage surely would not last,
Uh-uh, uh-uh."

Froggie said to Birdie, "Let us wed,
Oh please, oh please.
I will keep you happy and well fed.
Sweetie, make me proud and nod your head,
Oh please, oh please."

Birdie said, "I will not marry you,
No thanks, no thanks.
I would think about it if you flew,
But you smell of swamp; you're slimy too.
No thanks, no thanks."

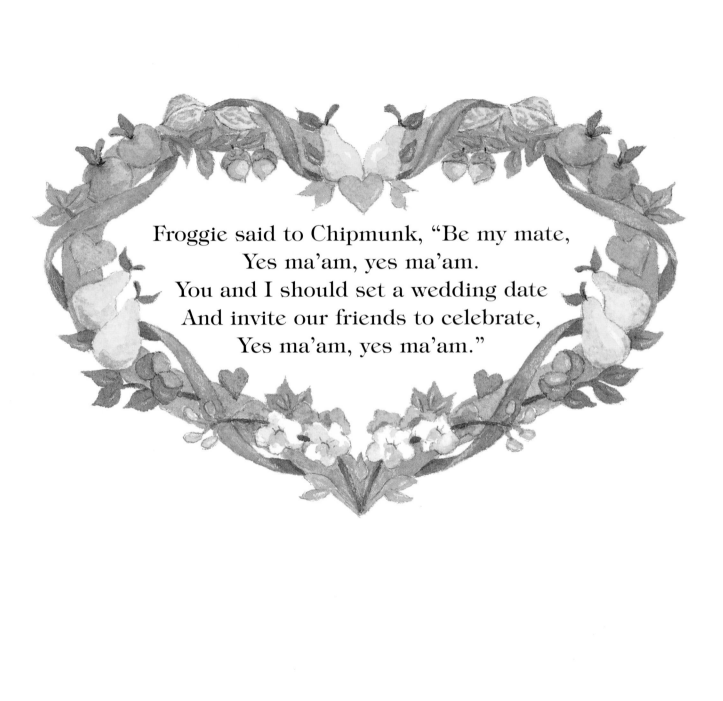

Froggie said to Chipmunk, "Be my mate,
Yes ma'am, yes ma'am.
You and I should set a wedding date
And invite our friends to celebrate,
Yes ma'am, yes ma'am."

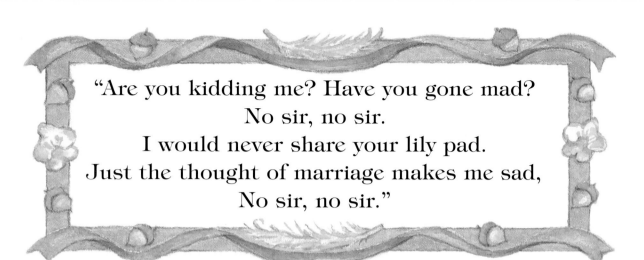

"Are you kidding me? Have you gone mad?
No sir, no sir.
I would never share your lily pad.
Just the thought of marriage makes me sad,
No sir, no sir."

Froggie saw a vision by the creek,
Oh my, oh my!
"Thump, thump" went his heart, his knees grew weak,
And his head did spin, he could not speak,
Oh my, oh my!

She said, "Froggie, will you marry me?
Yes yes, yes yes?
What a happy couple we will be.
I will cherish you, just wait and see.
Yes yes, yes yes!"

Froggie said, "My courtin' days are through."
Hooray! Hooray!
Joyfully he croaked, "I'll marry you!"
And they danced and hopped like froggies do!
Hooray! Hooray!

Froggie Went A-Courtin'

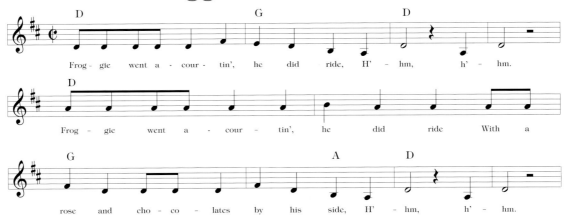

Frog - gie went a - cour - tin', he did ride, H' - hm, h' - hm.

Frog - gie went a - cour - tin', he did ride With a

rose and cho - co - lates by his side, H' - hm, h' - hm.

2. Froggie said to Mousie, "Marry me,
Oh yes, oh yes.
Be my little honey, my sweet pea;
What a caring husband I will be,
Oh yes, oh yes."

3. "I don't want a frog to hold and squeeze,
Oh no, oh no.
I don't like the water, you hate cheese,
So you might as well get off your knees,
Oh no, oh no."

4. Froggie said to Turtle, "Be my bride,
A-ha, a-ha.
Hurry up my darling do decide,
For a love like ours can't be denied,
A-ha, a-ha."

5. Turtle shook her head, "You move too fast,
Uh-uh, uh-uh.
We don't need an expert to forecast
That our marriage surely would not last,
Uh-uh, uh-uh."

6. Froggie said to Birdie, "Let us wed,
Oh please, oh please.
I will keep you happy and well fed.
Sweetie, make me proud and nod your head,
Oh please, oh please."

7. Birdie said, "I will not marry you,
No thanks, no thanks.
I would think about it if you flew,
But you smell of swamp; you're slimy too.
No thanks, no thanks."

8. Froggie said to Chipmunk, "Be my mate,
Yes ma'am, yes ma'am.
You and I should set a wedding date
And invite our friends to celebrate,
Yes ma'am, yes ma'am."

9. "Are you kidding me? Have you gone mad?
No sir, no sir.
I would never share your lily pad.
Just the thought of marriage makes me sad.
No sir, no sir."

10. Froggie saw a vision by the creek,
Oh my, oh my!
"Thump, thump" went his heart, his knees grew weak,
And his head did spin, he could not speak,
Oh my, oh my!

11. She said, "Froggie, will you marry me?
Yes yes, yes yes?
What a happy couple we will be.
I will cherish you, just wait and see.
Yes yes, yes yes!"

12. Froggie said, "My courtin' days are through."
Hooray! Hooray!
Joyfully he croaked, "I'll marry you!"
And they danced and hopped like froggies do!
Hooray! Hooray!